Christie and Agatha's DETECTIVE AGENCY

First published in the UK by Sweet Cherry Publishing Limited, 2024
Unit 36, Vulcan House, Vulcan Road,
Leicester, LE5 3EF, United Kingdom

Sweet Cherry Europe (Europe address)
Nauschgasse 4/3/2 POB 1017
Vienna, WI 1220, Austria

2 4 6 8 10 9 7 5 3 1

ISBN: 978-1-78226-819-2

Christie and Agatha's Detective Agency:
To Halt a Heist

Text by Pip Murphy
Illustrations by Roberta Tedeschi

www.sweetcherrypublishing.com

Printed and bound in Turkey

MIX
Paper from
responsible sources
FSC® C151955

Christie and Agatha's
DETECTIVE AGENCY

TO HALT A HEIST

Sweet Cherry

PIP MURPHY

Illustrated by
ROBERTA TEDESCHI

CHAPTER ONE

Christie and Agatha were now
famous. The twin sisters had
solved mysteries in England,
Scotland, Egypt and France. They
had found lost items, stopped
sabotage, located missing persons
and put an end to several nasty
plots. Their mother, Clara, had
already covered a large section of
their Torquay drawing-room wall

with framed newspaper clippings and letters of thanks from well-known figures such as Howard Carter, the Curie sisters and Albert Einstein.

Yet despite the young pair's glowing record, nobody had approached them for help directly. All of their cases had come to them via personal connections or chance. Their sponsor, Sir Conan Doyle, said he had placed advertisements for the girls' detective agency in all

CHRISTIE & AGATHA'S DETECTIVE AGENCY

Will solve any problem, big or small
(preferably big).

TORQUAY, ENGLAND, THE WORLD

the best newspapers. But so far they hadn't received so much as a single letter asking for their assistance.

Still, this didn't stop Christie from rushing to check the post every morning, just in case.

One particular morning, Christie was in the back garden when the post arrived. A marvellously long grass snake had moved in near their pond. If she tiptoed out early enough she could sometimes see it basking in the morning sun.

While Christie was crouched in the garden watching the timid snake, three adults were sitting in the drawing room watching Agatha.

Agatha gulped and turned shyly away from the onlooking eyes. The fond gaze of her mother was fine, but being observed by the visiting Sir Conan Doyle and their elderly neighbour Mrs Trellis brought her out in a cold sweat.

Then, to her relief, Christie burst into the drawing room. 'Good morning, Mother!' Noticing the guests, she added, 'Oh! Good morning, Mrs Trellis. Good morning, Sir Conan Doyle.' Her polite tone was let down by her appearance. Her blouse's sleeves were rolled up and there were grass stains and dirt on both her socks and skirt. The girls' friend Auguste would have been horrified at the sight. But Mrs Trellis was shocked enough in his absence.

'What on earth have you been doing, child?' she exclaimed.

'I was checking on the snake, Mrs Trellis,' answered Christie. She turned to Sir Conan Doyle, completely missing her neighbour's alarmed expression. 'Didn't you write a story about a snake once?' she asked.

'Indeed I did,' he said.

'What sort of snake was in your story?' Christie asked. 'I've got the most fantastic book on snakes that mother bought me for my last birthday. It's written by a woman, too. Her name is Miss Henrietta Buchanan.'

'It was a … swamp adder,' answered Sir Conan Doyle.

'A swamp adder,' repeated Christie. 'I don't think I remember seeing that one in the book. Where's it from?' Sir Conan Doyle gave an awkward cough. 'So,' he said, changing the subject and gesturing to the frame-filled wall next to him, 'I see that your detective agency has been a considerable success!'

'Yes,' said Christie simply. 'Oh golly, I just remembered that I didn't check the morning post for new clients. Did it come yet?'

'I think I heard it come through the letterbox a little while ago,' said Clara.

Christie fidgeted.

'Why don't you go and fetch it for me?' suggested Clara.

Christie didn't need asking twice. She was off like a rocket.

Mrs Trellis had just finished tutting and was taking a sip of tea when there came a sudden, loud cry from the hall.

One third of Mrs Trellis's tea remained in her cup. The second third of the tea splashed onto her face and up her nose. The final third spilt down the front of her cardigan. She was still spluttering when Christie, unaware of the chaos she had caused, raced back into the drawing room, waving a letter in the air.

'It's for us!' she cried to her
sister. 'For our detective agency!
We've got a new case!'

CHAPTER TWO

'Thank you for allowing me to join you,' said Auguste, in his polite Belgian accent.

'Of course!' said Christie. 'We wouldn't dream of going without you.'

Agatha nodded. After all, Auguste had been a vital part of most of their cases. Going off on this new adventure without him would be unthinkable.

It was the next day and the three children were crammed together in the back of Sir Conan Doyle's motor car, while their mother sat up front on the passenger side. The meeting with their client – Mr Bhatnagar – wasn't until the following morning, but Clara had said she thought it would be best to get there the day before. The great writer had offered to give them a lift up to London since he was going there himself anyway.

'Did we show you the presents that Mr Einstein sent us?' Christie asked Auguste. 'As a thank you for helping him with the train mystery.'

The boy shook his head. 'No. But he sent me a present, too: these green and bronze cufflinks. The colours of the Green Express.' He raised his hands so the girls could see them.

'How beautiful!' said Agatha.

'He kept the same colour scheme for our presents,' said Christie. She brought out a green-coloured electric torch with bronze ends. 'He wrote that it's "for investigating dark places". I bet it'll come in handy.'

'And he gave me this fountain pen,' said Agatha, holding up a gorgeous pen in matching colours. 'For writing about the mysteries we solve. I haven't used it yet, though. I thought I should wait until we had a new case.'

'And now you do!' said Auguste. 'Please tell me all about it.'

'Well,' said Christie, 'the client, Mr Bhatnagar, is worried for the safety of the device he invented called the Magnetic Interference Balance.'

Auguste looked confused. 'What is a Magnetic Interference Balance?'

'Um, he says in his letter that it's a device for measuring magnetic properties,' explained Agatha. 'Mr Bhatnagar is planning to exhibit it at the Royal Society Summer Science Exhibition in London. But he's received an anonymous letter warning him that someone is planning to steal it.'

'He was thinking about pulling out of the exhibition until he saw our advertisement in the newspaper and decided to ask for our help instead,' said Christie.

Auguste nodded. 'He will not regret his choice. I am sure your little grey brain cells will solve the matter for him.'

'I hope so,' said Agatha. 'Though I'm afraid it might be difficult to solve something that hasn't actually happened yet.'

She wasn't to know that it was the client, rather than the case itself, that would prove to be the biggest obstacle to their success.

Aside from their appointment with Mr Bhatnagar, the children

were more or less free to do as
they pleased in London. Agatha
was eager to visit some of the big
bookshops that the capital city
had to offer, while Christie and
Auguste wanted to look around the
British Museum.

Sir Conan Doyle said he had
some business to attend to, but he
would join them for lunch the next
day to hear the details of their new
case. So it was just Clara and the
children exploring by themselves.

After dropping off their luggage
at the cosy, family-run hotel, the
four of them took the Central

20

London Railway line and got off
at the British Museum station.
As they walked out of the grand
station building, Christie was
telling the others about a fantastic
new word that she had learnt from
her snake book: 'chore'. 'It says
that snakes chore eggs from birds'
nests,' she explained. 'Apparently
that means "steal" in Scottish.
We'll have to try it out on Sir Co–'

All of a sudden, the two girls
heard their names being called.

'Christie! Agatha!'

They turned their heads at the
shouting.

There, on the pavement opposite them, was a red-headed girl with a big grin on her face. She was waving at them energetically and her enthusiasm only grew when she saw that she'd caught their eye.

'Who's that, dear?' asked Clara.

'Nobody,' muttered Christie, pulling Agatha along by the hand. 'Keep walking.'

'She seems to know you,' their mother pointed out. 'She's heading towards us. She's about to cross— oh my goodness!'

A split second later the monotone rhythm of the street was broken by the frantic squeal of brakes.

CHAPTER THREE

Auguste and the two sisters gaped
at the grinning girl bounding the
last few steps to their side of the
pavement. She completely ignored
the furious drivers she had left
yelling in her wake.

'It's so wonderful
to see the three
of you again!'
she said.

25

'And you must be Christie and Agatha's mother. I'm Ada. Ada Lemon. It's a pleasure to meet you.'

'Likewise,' said Clara, smiling. 'Although I'd be careful crossing roads like that! I wouldn't want this to be our last meeting. By the way, if you don't mind me asking, how *do* you know each other?'

'Oh.' Ada looked disappointed. 'Didn't they tell you about me? We met in Egypt.'

'Of course!' Clara said at once. 'Silly me, forgetting like that.'

The twins both thought how nice their mother was to spare

the girl's hurt feelings. Christie, however, was still annoyed at Ada from their last meeting. She had deliberately complicated the mystery that they had been working on.

'What are you doing in London?' asked Agatha, before her sister could say anything rude.

'Staying with Daddy,' said Ada, pulling a face. 'He's usually far too important and unavailable to spend time with little old me. But all of his employees are busy doing real work today, so he didn't have much choice.'

As if on cue, an imposing late-middle-aged man with white hair and contrasting dark, bushy eyebrows appeared.

Like a badger! thought Christie.

'Please excuse my daughter,' the man said with a brisk nod. 'My name is Leonard Lemon.' He handed Clara a business card. 'You may have heard of my newspaper – the *Daily Rind*.'

'Goodness,' said Clara. 'Yes, of course we have.'

Christie quickly held out one of their own business cards. 'We're Christie and Agatha Parker,' she said, gesturing to herself and her sister. 'This is our mother, Clara, and our friend,

Auguste Dupont. You may have heard of *us*,' she added, imitating Mr Lemon's grand manner and tone.

Ada chuckled.

Mr Lemon gave Christie a suspicious look, wondering if she was mocking him, but Ada said, 'They have a monthly advertisement in your paper, Daddy.'

His expression cleared. 'Then I would like to offer you my thanks for selecting our newspaper in

which to place your advertisement.'
He gazed at the children
thoughtfully, then turned abruptly
to Clara. 'If you don't mind, Mrs
Parker, might I have a quick word
with your daughters?'

'If they don't object, then neither
do I,' said Clara. She assumed,
as did her daughters, that this
man was interested in making an
article about the twins and their
adventures.

The sisters followed Ada's father
a short way down the street.
Christie opened her mouth to
speak but before she could,

Mr Lemon said, 'How long will you be in London?'

'About a week, I think,' said Christie.

'Perfect. Can you keep an eye on Ada for the next few days? Entertain her, keep her out of mischief, that sort of thing?'

Christie blinked, taken aback. This wasn't about their detective agency?

'Er, yes, I suppose so,' said Agatha, recovering more quickly than her sister. 'Apart from tomorrow morning. We've got an appointment then.'

'That's fine. You can start after that.' Mr Lemon produced a fat wallet from inside his jacket and pulled out a pile of cash. 'How much do you want? Five pounds? Ten?'

The twins stared at him.

'What are you giving us money for?' asked Christie in alarm.

'Come on,' said Mr Lemon impatiently. 'We all know how difficult Ada can be. What's your price for pretending to be her friend for the rest of the week?'

Christie glared at him. 'Nothing!' she snapped.

'Oh, come on. Just name your price and be done with it.'

'I *said* nothing,' repeated Christie through gritted teeth, 'because we're not pretending to be anything! We *are* her friends. And she can join us today for nothing, too!'

Agatha nodded her head earnestly.

Mr Lemon gave them a strange look, then shrugged and put his wallet away. 'So be it,' he said. 'She's all yours.'

And with that, he gave a curt nod in the direction of the others and walked briskly away.

Clara and Auguste looked after the man in confusion.

'He left in rather a hurry, didn't he?' said Clara. 'You didn't say anything to upset him, did you, Chrissie?'

'Not really,' said Christie.

'He was just asking if Ada could spend the rest of the day with us,' said Agatha. 'And, er, the rest of the week, actually. Do you mind?'

'Of course not,' said Clara. 'That would be lovely.'

'So, how much did he give you?' asked Ada, when Clara had gone to use the bathroom at the museum.

The girls stared at her in surprise and Ada laughed.

'You needn't look so shocked. That's what he always does. Every

school holiday he pays some kids
in my class to pretend to be friends
with me.'

'He pays them?' repeated
Auguste, horrified.

'Yes. Sometimes he pays their
parents, too, and packs me off to
their house. I usually manage
to run away before the end of the
holidays, though.'

How awful, thought Agatha.
'He didn't give us anything at all,'
she said.

'He offered,' admitted Christie,
'but we didn't take it.'

'Goodness, why ever not?' asked

Ada. 'Just think of all the chocolate we could have bought.'

'Because we want you to know that we really *are* your friends,' said Agatha. 'Nobody has to pay us to spend time with you. We want to.'

'Of course!' said Auguste.

'More or less,' muttered Christie. She didn't want Ada to think that she'd forgiven her for the problems she'd caused last time.

'Oh,' said Ada. It was her turn to look surprised. 'Thanks.' Then, grinning like a Cheshire cat, she added, 'But I still think you should have taken his money.'

CHAPTER FOUR

The next day, Christie, Agatha and Auguste all had a positive impression of Mr Bhatnagar when he opened the door to greet them. Auguste noted his neat toothbrush moustache with satisfaction. Agatha was relieved by his kindly face. Christie was encouraged by the twinkle in his eyes.

Unfortunately, Mr Bhatnagar's

impression of them seemed less positive. As his gaze travelled downwards to his young callers, his face fell.

'Sorry, can I help you children with something?' he asked.

'Actually, *we're* going to be the ones to help *you*,' said Christie. She thrust one of her business cards at the man. He took it, looking puzzled.

'You mean to say … well, er, please come in.'

'I'm Christie and this is my sister, Agatha,' Christie explained as the man guided them to the small sitting room. 'And this is our friend, Auguste. Don't worry, we've solved plenty of crimes that *have* happened so we shouldn't have any trouble stopping one that hasn't.'

'I see.' The man nodded, but he still looked uneasy. 'And will your parents be joining us?'

'No,' said Christie.

'Mother's reading a book in a café. We are then going for lunch next door at The Mayfair restaurant. So we have until then to discuss the case.'

Mr Bhatnagar nodded again and gestured to the sofas. 'Well, since you've come all this way, please do sit down. Would you care for tea and biscuits?'

As their new client began to pour the tea, Auguste asked, 'Do you live in London, Mr Bhatnagar?'

'No, actually. This place belongs to my friend and colleague, Mr

Mathur. He's been kind enough to let me stay here while I'm in England for the Royal Society exhibition. I'm currently working as a professor at the Punjab University.'

'Very impressive,' said Christie. 'Teaching magnetics?'

'Yes, my expertise is in various areas of chemistry. Would you like milk and sugar?'

After a few minutes of polite chit-chat, Christie thought it was high time to get down to business. 'You said that you had received a letter warning you that someone is going to steal your magnetic balance device?'

'Magnetic Interference Balance, yes. I have the letter here, if you want to see it.'

'Yes, please,' replied Agatha.

The children frowned at the piece of paper intently. The word choice was interesting. 'It says that someone is going to "chore" your device unless you pull out of the exhibition,' said Christie.

'Yes,' said Mr Bhatnagar. 'It's a Scottish word meaning "steal".'

'We know,' said Christie. 'But that must narrow the pool of suspects, surely.'

'Do you have any idea whom the

letter might have been from?' asked Auguste.

'No, I'm afraid not. I didn't recognise the handwriting.'

Agatha pulled out her new fountain pen and wrote in her notebook 'anonymous tip off – still anonymous'.

'Well, do you have any rival inventors?' asked Christie.

'No, I've always had good relations with my fellow researchers. My projects are often based on meeting a particular need rather than trying to make a name for myself. So I don't tend to clash with people.'

'Um, if you don't mind me asking,' said Agatha, nervously crumbling her biscuit, 'if there's nobody you're at odds with, then could the warning just be a practical joke?'

Mr Bhatnagar hesitated. 'It is possible, yes.'

'But you think not?' said Auguste.

'During my time studying in London I encountered a great deal of kindness. However, there were some people who were not so pleasant to those from backgrounds different to their own. One fellow

46

student in particular, Sir Anthony
Bullock, tried to ridicule me and
my countrymen whenever he could.
Although, luckily, most people chose
to ignore him.'

'They should have told him to
stop, not just ignored him,' said
Christie severely. She was about to
say more when their client suddenly
put down his teacup.

'I'm so sorry,' said Mr Bhatnagar. 'I
think I might have made a mistake.'

'Please don't worry,' said Auguste.
'These girls are most discreet. I am
sure there will be no trouble from
revealing the man's name.'

'Ah, no, what I mean is that I think I made a mistake in asking for your help.'

The children stared at him.

'You mean you don't want us to investigate after all?' asked Christie. 'But what about that Bullock fellow?'

'No, I don't think it will be necessary,' said Mr Bhatnagar. 'Saying all of this out loud has made me realise how foolish I've been.'

'But–' Christie began. Their would-be client hastily continued before she could protest further.

'I'm so sorry to have wasted your time,' he said. 'I will of course repay your travel costs. But you don't need to investigate further.'

An awkward silence followed, broken only by the clink of the teacups. None of them had expected such an abrupt rejection.

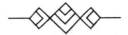

Three dejected children left the building ten minutes later. They had barely trudged a few yards away from the door, however, when a voice hailed them.

'I wouldn't go in there, if I were you!'

They turned to see a short,

stocky young man with a sickly complexion and pale blue eyes set in a deep frown.

Too down to care who this newcomer was, Christie said, 'I wouldn't worry. I don't think

we're likely to be going back there. We're not wanted.'

'Well, in that case I – I being Albert Butcher, by the way – would say you've had a narrow escape,' said the young man.

'Who knows what those two might have done to you otherwise. Used you as guinea pigs, no doubt.'

What on earth was he talking about? They stared at him in confusion. Even Christie started to regain a small spark of interest. After all, this sounded exactly like something straight out of the adventure books she enjoyed.

'Sorry, who might have used us as guinea pigs and for what?' asked Agatha.

'Those Mathur and Bhatnagar fellows.' Mr Butcher glanced dramatically from side to side.

Deciding that the coast was clear, he reached into his satchel and produced a booklet that he held out to the children.

Agatha took it. 'The Royal Society Summer Science Exhibition,' she read aloud.

The man bobbed his head up and down energetically. 'Exactly!' he said. 'Now if you turn to page eight–' Agatha did so, '–you'll see that there is a device listed there, invented by those two scoundrels, that is described as a "Magnetic Interference Balance".'

53

'Yes,' said Auguste. 'It is a device for measuring magnetic properties.'

'Ha!' scoffed the young man. 'That's what they *want* you to think! But what does "interference" mean? It means that the device interferes with people's brainwaves, that's what! They're trying to control people's minds!'

There was a short silence.

'Isn't "interference" something to do with how magnets mess up compasses?' said Christie.

'And, um, I think if they were trying to control people's minds,' said Agatha, 'I'm not sure that they'd advertise it in the product's title.'

The man's frown deepened.
He drew himself up to his full
height, which was not terribly
impressive. 'I see,' he muttered to
himself. 'They've got to you already.
The device is clearly effective on
children, at least. I had better be on
my guard!'

The children watched Albert
Butcher hurry away.

'Well,' said Agatha, 'I think we
have at least two suspects now.'

Christie's shoulders slumped.
'You're right,' she said. 'I only wish
we had a case!'

CHAPTER FIVE

The grandness of The Mayfair was not enough to restore Christie's high spirits at lunch.

'Goodness me, why the long faces?' asked Sir Conan Doyle. 'Did something happen?'

'Are you all right?' asked Clara, standing up to give her girls a hug.

'I am afraid that the girls' new case did not quite work out,' said

Auguste with a sigh.

'It didn't work out?' repeated Sir Conan Doyle. 'Whatever do you mean? Nobody could expect you to completely solve everything in only a few hours.'

'He doesn't want us to solve it at all,' said Christie glumly, detaching herself from her mother and taking a seat at the table.

'Oh dear,' said Clara. 'Well, let's eat first. Then you can tell us all about what happened, and we can see what can be done about it.'

Once the children had finished eating bowlfuls of vegetables and boatloads of gravy, and were starting to tuck into their desserts, Clara asked, 'So, what happened with Mr Bhatnagar?'

'He backed out in the middle of our interview and sent us packing, that's what happened!' groaned Christie.

'Bhatnagar,' repeated Sir Conan Doyle. 'From what I've heard he's a very impressive chap and an extremely nice fellow. He's received dozens of awards and thank-you gifts for his work, but he always donates a great part of his earnings to his university for funding

research.' He poured cream over
his apple pie. 'Apparently he said
nobody ever trusts a scientist who's
purely after money. It's the selfless

ones who are the most trustworthy and inspirational.'

'So what was the problem?' asked Clara. 'Why did he send you away like that?'

'I think he might have thought we're too young,' said Agatha. 'He *did* look rather taken aback when he saw us.'

Sir Conan Doyle shook his head. 'But Mr Bhatnagar himself was a prodigy in both science and literature! Surely it would be ridiculous for him to worry about your age if he himself showed such early talent?'

'Perhaps he's worried about your safety,' said Clara.

Christie paused in the demolition of her sticky toffee pudding. 'Actually, you might be right. He was antsy from the start. But it wasn't until I said people should take a stand against bullies that he kicked us off the case.'

'Were you referring to any bully in particular?' asked Clara.

'He mentioned a man from his student days,' said Auguste. 'Sir Anthony Bullock. Have you heard of him?'

'I have indeed,' said Sir

Conan Doyle, 'but nothing good. He inherited his fortune and title at a young age and apparently that caused his head to swell with arrogance. By all accounts it didn't swell from the size of his brain.' He chuckled.

'If he's not very clever then he isn't likely to be that dangerous, *is* he?' said Christie.

Sir Conan Doyle sipped his tea. 'I wish that were the case,' he said. 'Sadly, the genius villain generally exists only in the world of fiction. In real life it is most often the powerful idiots with overinflated egos that one must be wary of. I can understand why Mr Bhatnagar would be concerned at the idea of you crossing Bullock.'

'Is he Scottish?' asked Christie suddenly, thinking of the wording in the warning letter.

Sir Conan Doyle raised his eyebrows. 'No, but he did grow up on his family's Scottish estate, I believe. Although how you guessed that, given he has such an English name, I couldn't imagine!'

'Using her little grey brain cells,' said Auguste proudly.

'What will you do next?' asked

Sir Conan Doyle. 'Would you like me to go and have a word with Mr Bhatnagar? Explain that we can keep you out of harm's way and help you with the case?'

'No, you don't need to do that,' said Christie. 'I'd like to solve it ourselves, if we can. That way it means more.' She ate a few more mouthfuls of pudding. 'I'm just not sure what we *can* do if we're not officially on the case.'

'Erm, actually,' said Agatha, fiddling with the edge of the tablecloth, 'I might have an idea. But I think we'll need Ada's help.'

CHAPTER SIX

Anyone watching the four children sitting in the snug, quiet café a few hours later would never have guessed that the afternoon tea wasn't their first meal of the day. They tucked into the bottom layer of sandwiches with gusto.

The café had been Ada's suggestion, after the other three told her that they had something important to discuss. In Auguste's disapproving opinion the place looked more like a cluttered library than a café. It had low, worn leather sofas and its walls lined with a jumble of disorganised books. Agatha thought it was wonderful.

To take his mind off the untidiness, Auguste explained their problem to Ada.

'In summary,' he said, 'someone will probably try to steal Mr Bhatnagar's Magnetic Interference Balance from the Royal Society–' He broke off in horror as he watched Ada casually take one of the macarons from the top tier. 'What are you doing?' he asked. 'In your English afternoon tea, you eat the sandwiches first, then the scones, then the little sweets.'

'Yes,' agreed Ada. 'But I felt like a macaron.'

'Erm, anyway,' said Agatha. 'Our idea was that we could maybe get to the exhibition first and move the device *before* it gets taken.'

'Excellent,' said Ada. 'When are we stealing it?'

'We're not stealing it!' snapped

Christie, who was starting to make headway into the scones. The jam lining the corners of her mouth made her scowl look even more fearsome. 'We're stopping the theft. We're rescuing it.'

'Excellent,' said Ada. 'When are we rescuing it?'

'The exhibition starts tomorrow so I think the only time we – and the thief, for that matter – *can* do it is tonight,' said Agatha. She bit her lip. 'But as we haven't officially been given permission to help, we're probably going to have to be a bit, er, quiet about taking it.'

'I'm curious,' said Ada, grinning at Christie. 'You say we're not stealing it, but what *would* you call taking someone's device without permission?'

'We're not going to take it anywhere far. We're just going to move it somewhere else inside the venue and then watch to see who turns up to steal it.'

'It made me think a bit of what you did in Egypt,' Agatha explained, 'so I thought you would be a good person to ask for help.'

Ada looked pleased. 'Well, I'm happy to be involved,' she said.

'Let's see. The first thing is to let your mother know we are going to be out late doing research for the case.

Ada ate another macaron, then reached down to the scone layer. Auguste looked on in disapproving silence. 'Now, fill me in on the suspects,' she said. 'I'm assuming you already have some.'

'There are two,' said Auguste. 'Mr Albert Butcher and Sir Anthony Bullock.'

They told Ada all about the two men in between mouthfuls of scones and sweets.

'So one's a fool and the other's a bully,' stated Ada, when they had finished. 'I see. This should be fun. Let's meet up in the foyer outside of the exhibition hall at about six o'clock. You lot take your time.'

'Wouldn't it be easier for us all to go there together?' asked Auguste.

'It would,' Ada agreed, 'if I didn't have some preparations to make on the way. Besides, you need to speak to your mother first.' She popped the final macaron into her mouth with a wink and sprang up from the table. 'See you there!' she called back over her shoulder. 'Don't be late!'

The twins and Auguste stood a little way away from the exhibition hall, watching all the people bustling about. About two thirds of them were clearly staff and porters. Some of whom looked almost as young as themselves. While the remaining third were probably the exhibitors making some last-minute adjustments.

Auguste checked his beloved pocket watch. 'It is almost six o'clock,' he said.

A moment later this was confirmed by the loud bongs of a nearby clock.

As the chimes faded away, the children glanced around.

'Ada did say to meet at six,' said Christie, forgetting she herself was often late. 'Where *is* she?'

'Right here, guv'nor,' said a hoarse voice next to them.

All three of them jumped, then stared in surprise at the speaker. At first glance it appeared to

be one of the boys who'd been
helping to carry the boxes into the
exhibition hall. But then the cap
tilted back to reveal a mess of red
hair and freckles.

'Hello, gang,' Ada grinned.
'Ready for a spot of disguise?
We need to find somewhere to
change before we can go into the
exhibition hall.'

CHAPTER SEVEN

Disguises on, it was surprisingly
easy to sneak into the exhibition
hall. All they had to do was walk
up, caps pulled low over their eyes,
grab hold of some of the boxes and
haul them inside.

The children had agreed to
split into pairs once they were
through the door. This way they
could make their way to the

meeting point without drawing any unwanted attention. The large main room was overlooked by an upper balcony. The meeting point was a door leading up to the balcony that Ada had earmarked as their hideout.

'How do you know about it?' Christie asked her.

'I've been there before,' said Ada. 'And it's always good to notice these things.'

Fearing that Ada being paired with Auguste or her sister might lead to conflict, Agatha volunteered to go with the red-headed girl herself. She was still worried, though. She thought that at any second somebody was going to point at her and declare, 'She doesn't belong here!' and then drag her and the others off to the police station. But the cry of accusation never came. They were, as Ada had said they would be, mostly ignored.

Christie, naturally, was having the time of her life. She had never been in a *real* disguise before, only fancy dress.

'Where would you like this one, guv'nor?' Christie asked a nearby staff member in her gruffest voice,

indicating the box in her arms
with a nod of her capped head.

'Oh, just over there,' said the
man. He barely gave her a first
glance as he pointed, let alone a
second one. Christie grinned. This
was too exciting for words!

Agatha and Ada were intrigued
by the exhibits taking shape as
they passed. There were heaps
of test tubes, glass cases, tiny
devices and heavy machinery.
Unfortunately, Agatha was so
distracted by a display entitled
'Solving Crimes Through Science'
that she stumbled over a box that

had been left lying in one of the aisles. She would have ended up sprawled on the floor had Ada not grabbed her arm just in time.

'Can't you look where you're going?' snapped a tall man with pale blue eyes, glaring at her. 'You nearly landed on my foot!'

'Sorry!' mumbled Agatha.

It was then that she realised she'd dropped her fountain pen on the floor. She reached down to pick it up, but the tall man was quicker than she was and snatched it up off the ground.

'Erm, sorry, but could I have it back?' asked Agatha.

'I think not,' the man sneered at her, slipping it into the pocket of his jacket. 'This is clearly far too expensive a thing for a scoundrel like you.'

'But it was a present!' protested Agatha.

'Stolen, you mean,' said the man. 'As if someone would give a present like that to a scruffy child. Run along now, before I call a constable!'

The police! Agatha swallowed. While the pen was rightfully hers, getting the police involved could prove disastrous! What if they were thrown out of the exhibition before they could safely move Mr Bhatnagar's device?

'All right,' said Ada. 'We'll go.' She sounded calm but as she took Agatha's hand and led her away, Agatha could see that Ada's green eyes were sparkling with anger.

''Scuse me,' said Ada to a passing member of staff. 'Who is that tall gent with the pale eyes?'

The woman glanced in the direction Ada was pointing. 'Oh, that's Sir Anthony Bullock,' she said with a frown. 'I'd steer clear of him if I were you! *Not* a gentleman, in my opinion.'

'Thanks,' said Ada. As the woman left, however, Ada grinned at Agatha, giving her hand a squeeze. 'Perhaps Sir Anthony should steer clear of *us*!'

Meanwhile, Christie and Auguste had spied a friendlier face. Unfortunately, it was also one they didn't want to see at that precise moment.

'Oh no!' hissed Christie. 'It's Mr Bhatnagar. Quick!'

She and Auguste turned on the spot at once and began walking

briskly in the other direction.
They hurried around the corner of
the row of tables, colliding with a
stocky lady coming the other way
as they did so.

'Oh, I'm so sorry,' she said in
a soft lilting voice. 'I should pay
more attention.'

'As should we,' replied Auguste
politely.

Christie, however, stared at the
lady with wide eyes. 'I say, you're
not Miss Henrietta Buchanan, are
you?' she gasped.

The lady looked even more
astonished than Christie. 'I am!' she

said. 'However did you know that?'

'She is a detective,' said Auguste.

'And I read your book,' said Christie. 'The one on snakes. There was a picture of you on the dust jacket.'

'Oh my goodness!' said Miss Buchanan, looking flustered. 'I have to admit, this is the first time that anybody has recognised me. If you want to become popular, writing about snakes is certainly not the right way to go about it.'

'I don't know why not!' said Christie. 'It's a fantastic book. Although if you do make another edition, you might want to include

something about swamp adders.
I couldn't find anything about them
in your book.'

The lady laughed. 'I'm not sure
you can find anything about them in
any book, except Sir Conan Doyle's,'
she said. 'He made them up.'

Christie was taken aback. *No
wonder he changed the subject so
quickly when I asked about them!*
she thought to herself. She saw
Auguste looking pointedly at the
hall clock and sighed. 'I'm afraid
we've got to go now, but will you
be here tomorrow? I'd love it if you
could sign my book.'

Miss Buchanan blushed. 'Well, yes, I will, and I would be most honoured to sign your book. Until tomorrow, then!'

'I think you put quite the spring in her step,' said Auguste, as they made their way to the meeting place. 'I think maybe her work does not get much attention.'

'No,' agreed Christie. 'Snakes are so misunderstood, aren't they? It's such a shame.'

They hurried over to join the other two, who were waiting innocently by the door leading to the upper floor. As soon as they

arrived, Ada grasped the handle
and turned it, ushering the others
inside before following herself.

'I can't believe they would leave it unlocked like that,' said Auguste.

Ada's look of innocence became positively radiant.

She didn't pick the lock, did she? Christie wondered.

Before she could ask, Ada started up the stairs. 'I don't know about you lot,' Ada said over her shoulder, 'but I'm starving. Let's get into position on the balcony. Then we can nibble on some shortbread while Agatha and I tell you about our encounter with the awful Sir Anthony Bullock.'

CHAPTER EIGHT

It was nightfall and the last of the exhibitors and staff were leaving.

While the friends waited and polished off Ada's shortbread, Agatha busied herself by writing down some notes about people's appearances – sadly with her pencil, rather than her wonderful fountain pen. It might come in useful for describing characters in her own stories.

'There really are a lot of people with beards, aren't there?' Agatha remarked aloud.

'Having facial hair does give one a scholarly appearance,' said Auguste. 'I think it is the hallmark of professorship.'

'What, even for the women?' said Ada with a grin.

Auguste bowed his head. 'I do apologise. I was not thinking of the female professors.'

'I wish there were more of them,' said Christie. 'I think it must be jolly tough for women to get accepted in the academic world, like Miss Buchanan.'

'There is a female Egyptologist at the University College of this city,' said Auguste. 'Miss Margaret Murray. My mother consulted with her for the Egyptian history book that she was writing.'

'London's a bit ahead of some of the other British cities,' said Ada. 'Did you know that the University of London was the first university in Britain to give degrees to women?' She glanced back down at the stragglers. 'Oh, there's a good beard, Auguste. What do you think?'

The others followed her gaze.
A figure with a very symmetrical
beard was wheeling a large
container across the hall.

'Indeed,' said Auguste. 'That
man's beard is most satisfactory.'

'All right,' said Christie, about
twenty minutes later. 'It looks
like the coast is clear now. But it's
certainly dark in here without the
lights. It's lucky we've got my new
electric torch.' She flourished it.

'Very nice,' said Ada. 'It looks like
a good one.'

'It was a gift from a client,' said Christie, unable to resist the boast. 'Aggie got a matching fountain pen. She'll have to show you later.'

Her sister looked down at her feet. While she and Ada had told the others about meeting Sir Anthony Bullock, they had left out the part about him stealing Agatha's pen. Agatha had been worried that Christie would storm off to confront him.

Ada patted her on the shoulder. 'Don't worry,' she whispered. 'I'm sure you'll get it back.'

The children crept silently back down the staircase, Christie leading the way with her torch. It was a good thing she had it – someone had left a lot of big boxes near the foot of the staircase and without the torch they might have fallen over them.

When they reached the bottom, however, Auguste frowned. 'Those windows are big. I think perhaps we might have to do without your fantastic torch, Chrissie.'

'He's right,' said Ada. 'Someone will probably see the light from the street and call the police.'

Reluctantly, Christie put her torch in her pocket.

When their eyes had adjusted to the darkness, Ada opened the door and they sneaked quietly back into the main hall. There was just enough light coming in from the streetlights for them to make out vague shapes. The room was full of mysterious looking rows of objects.

'Do you remember where Mr Bhatnagar's device was?' Christie asked Auguste. If anyone was going to remember details like that, it would be him.

'I think it was this way,' said Auguste.

As one, they tiptoed after him. However, when Auguste came to a halt, there was nothing resembling a device on the table in front of them. There was just a glass case filled with ...

'Goodness' whispered Christie. 'Just look at those snakes!'

'Ugh,' said Auguste, swiftly putting some distance between himself and the reptiles. He shook his head. 'I do not understand it. I thought this was where Mr Bhatnagar was standing earlier, next to some enormous device.'

'Perhaps it's on the opposite side?' suggested Agatha.

They looked. Nothing but test tubes.

'Hmm,' said Christie. 'Well, don't worry Auguste, your memory can't be right all the time.'

Auguste looked hurt.

'We could try splitting up to hunt for it,' said Ada. 'And signal to the others when we've found it.'

Nodding in agreement, they walked in opposite directions.

There's something funny about those snakes, Agatha thought to herself. If only she could work out

what it was that was bothering
her! She glanced back over her
shoulder at the snake case for
inspiration – which was why she
didn't see the stealthy figure
creeping towards her from the
other direction.

CHAPTER NINE

Agatha and the figure collided.
Agatha, being smaller and lighter,
bounced back and landed heavily
on her backside. Too astonished
and winded to speak, she merely
stared up at the dark figure who
had knocked her to the floor.
Despite having come off the better
for their encounter, the figure gave
a strangled cry of alarm, tripping

backwards into the table behind him.

Or at least, Agatha *thought* it was a he. Given that the other person was wearing a balaclava that covered their hair and most of their face, with a long, loose black coat, oversized black boots and black gloves, she wasn't entirely sure. The small portion of face that was exposed was extremely pale, right down to the watery blue eyes. If it wasn't for the fact that she had already run into his decidedly solid body, Agatha might have wondered if he was a ghost.

However, the way he clumsily sent a set of glass beakers crashing to the floor was definitely very *un*ghost-like. As was his second shrill shriek of panic.

'What's going on?' she heard Christie yell.

Oh dear! thought Agatha. *The police will definitely come if this mayhem keeps up.*

Perhaps it would be best to show the figure her face to reassure him. Removing the cap, she put on her best smile. 'Hello,' she said, 'I didn't mean to startle you, but–'

The third shriek was definitely the loudest. Screeching as if pursued by a whole army of ghosts or snakes, or both, the man turned and ran for his life.

Agatha watched him go, open-mouthed. She heard the outer door bang loudly as the figure pelted out of the building.

At that moment the others reached her.

'Are you all right?' Christie asked her at once.

'What happened?' asked Ada.

'Er, I'm not entirely sure,' said Agatha. 'I think I scared someone.'

'The thief?' asked Auguste.

'Maybe.' Although Agatha felt like a thief should be a little braver than that.

'Right!' said Christie, switching on her torch. 'After him!' She ran towards the door, crunching over the broken glass as she went, the others hot on her heels. Flinging open the door, the girl raised her torch – only to be blinded by a much bigger, brighter one.

They all gasped, covering their eyes.

'Now, what do we have here then?' came a slow, reliable voice.

It could be nobody other than a police officer. 'How many of you *are* there?'

A frantic voice said, 'They're not with me! It's those children that Bhatnagar and Mathur have mind-controlled to do their bidding!' *And that*, thought Christie, Agatha and Auguste, *could be nobody other than Mr Albert Butcher.*

None of the children, aside from the naturally nervous Agatha, had expected to end the night in a police station. But there they were, and on the wrong side of the law too.

'Now,' said the local inspector, looking down his nose at them sternly. 'I don't believe for a moment any of that nonsense that Mr Butcher is spouting, about mind control and the like, but I *do* believe you were messing around inside a place you had no right to be. What do you have to say for yourselves?'

Christie took a deep breath. They *had* been breaking the law. Would they end up locked in the Tower of London?

Before she could answer, however, someone else spoke up.

'We did have a right to be there, actually,' said Ada, grinning. 'Or at

CHRISTIE & AGATHA'S DETECTIVE AGENCY

Will solve any problem, big or small (preferably big).

TORQUAY, ENGLAND, THE WORLD

least, we were asked to be there by one of the exhibitors. Show him your business card, Chrissie. Is it okay for me to call you and Agatha by your nicknames, now that we are friends?"

'Of course!' replied Christie and Agatha together.

Ada smiled as Christie handed the policeman one of their cards. The man's bushy eyebrows rose. 'Detectives?' he said. 'You are children?'

'Aggie and Chrissie are the detectives,' said Ada modestly.

'Auguste and I are merely helping them. Why don't you show him Mr Bhatnagar's letter, Aggie? That should clear things up.'

Agatha rooted in her bag and produced the letter that Mr Bhatnagar had sent them. The policeman read it. 'Hmm. But this Mr Bhatnagar only asks you for a consultation here. How do I know that he asked you to hide out in the exhibition hall and wait for the thief?'

'Ask him,' said Ada grandly,

leaning back in her chair. 'I'm sure he'll confirm our story.'

'Very well,' said the police officer. 'I'll call your bluff and do just that. Please wait here.'

'I'm not sure he *will* confirm our story,' Christie whispered to Ada, while the police officer was out of the room. 'What makes you think he'll back us up? You've not even met him!'

'No,' admitted Ada. 'But you did say he's a nice person. I don't think he'd want you to be punished for trying to help him.'

'I hope you're right,' said Auguste,

thinking of what his parents would say if they heard that he had been held in a police station.

After what seemed like an eternity, the police officer returned. His expression looked very grim.

'It seems like I owe you two apologies.'

Even Ada looked surprised at this. 'Two?' she said.

'Yes. One for doubting your story, which Mr Bhatnagar has been good enough to confirm, even at this late hour.'

Phew! thought the children.

'And the second for mistakenly

taking you away from your task. I sent one of my constables over to check on the exhibition hall while I contacted Mr Bhatnagar and he has just returned. Unfortunately, it seems that the thief used the opportunity of your absence to strike. The Magnetic Interference Balance device has gone.'

CHAPTER TEN

'You did your best,' Mr Bhatnagar told the children over breakfast the next morning. He had asked them to meet him at a café near the exhibition hall. 'Thank you so much for trying, even after I'd asked you not to.'

'I can see why you did,' said Agatha. She looked down at the tablecloth. 'That Bullock man was quite scary.'

'He must have been the one to steal your device, too,' said Christie, buttering her toast with an air of frustration. 'That Butcher chap said he *wanted* to remove it, but he couldn't find it in the dark. If only we hadn't left! We should have known Bullock was up to something when we saw him there.'

'Well, as unpleasant as he might be, he *is* allowed to be there as a member of the Royal Society,' said Mr Bhatnagar.

Christie shook her head. 'But he didn't have an exhibit, right, Aggie? I don't remember his name being in the booklet Mr Butcher gave us. I'm sure we'd have noticed.'

'No, I'm pretty sure it wasn't.'

'Well, there you g–'

'The snakes!' Agatha gasped suddenly.

The others looked at her in surprise. It wasn't like her to interrupt, nor was it like her to speak so loudly.

'What about the snakes?' asked Christie.

'They weren't in that booklet either. I'm sure of it. I read it cover to cover and

I don't remember ever seeing anything about snakes.'

Auguste wiped his mouth with his napkin. 'And yet they *were* there,' he said. 'Right next to where Mr Bhatnagar's device should have been.'

Agatha rummaged through her bag and laid the booklet down on the table. Together, they poured over the contents. When they reached the back cover,

Ada grinned. 'You're quite right, Aggie. Well remembered. I wonder what that means?'

Christie thoughtfully rubbed her chin. 'This booklet was printed in advance, right? Do you think it's possible the snake thing was a late addition?'

'Hmm. I'm not sure The Royal Society Summer Science Exhibition would make a last-minute change like that,' said Ada.

'No,' said Mr Bhatnagar. 'I don't believe they would.'

They exchanged excited looks. This inconsistency *must* be important!

Then Agatha said, 'Oh! I've just had a thought. What if the reason that neither Mr Butcher nor we could find it was because it was already missing?'

'But surely we'd have noticed if someone had come in and taken

it,' said Auguste. 'Or at least heard them.'

Christie clapped her hands together. 'They might have done it earlier, when there were still people about. They could have disguised themselves as a member of staff and wheeled it straight out the door.'

Mr Bhatnagar shook his head. 'I was making adjustments almost until the end. There can't have been more than a dozen people still there when I left.'

The children considered this.

'The only person I remember

moving something big around after you left was that man with the pleasing beard,' said Auguste finally. 'But he was taking large boxes *into* the hall, not out of it.'

'And after that, big boxes appeared at the bottom of the staircase, just through that side door!' exclaimed Christie, excitedly. 'We were planning to move the device somewhere else in the venue, weren't we, to stop someone from stealing it? Well, what if this bearded person just moved it somewhere else too? Moved it to make space for their own exhibit!'

Auguste looked confused. 'But the exhibit of the snakes belongs to that lady you were talking to, doesn't it? The one who wrote that book you like. Who was the man with the beard, who performed the switch? Was it her accomplice?'

'I think,' said Ada, with her usual grin, 'that beards might be the hallmark of *women* scholars, too. At least fake beards.'

'Come on,' cried Christie, jumping to her feet. 'Let's get back to the exhibition, Mr Bhatnagar. There's still time to fix this!'

CHAPTER ELEVEN

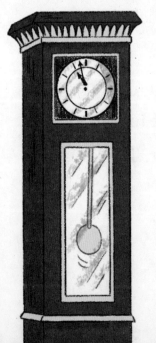

The five of them ran towards the exhibition hall at a speed Auguste considered to be most undignified. Panting, the children waited for Mr Bhatnagar to explain to the exhibition staff who he was and why they needed entry before the official

124

opening time of eleven o'clock.

'But *they're* not exhibitors,' the member of staff said, pointing at the children.

Mr Bhatnagar grinned. 'No,' he said. 'They are the detectives I hired to stop the theft of my Magnetic Interference Balance before the exhibition starts.'

Christie and Agatha's hearts swelled with pride.

Mr Bhatnagar glanced at his watch. 'And I believe they might well have managed it, too.'

Once inside, the group walked briskly towards the table where

Mr Bhatnagar's Magnetic Interference Balance should have been.

Miss Henrietta Buchanan was arranging a set of leaflets at the side of the display case when they approached. Spotting their reflection in the glass tank, she looked up and met their gaze.

'Ah,' she said, with a resigned nod. 'The detective girl and Mr Bhatnagar, I assume. I see that the game is up.'

Her accepting manner threw them off.

'So you admit to moving my device?' asked Mr Bhatnagar.

'Yes,' said Miss Buchanan. 'Sorry about that. Nothing personal, you understand. But I was starting to get a little desperate. Year after year my requests for an exhibit showing the effects of ultraviolet light on snakes have been rejected. Then finally, this year they said yes – but they changed their minds at the last minute. "There won't be enough space after all," they said. So I thought, well, why don't I *make* space then? So I did. I sent you a letter warning you that your device might be chored, in the hope that you'd drop out and I'd get my place back. But when that didn't work, I thought I might as well just move it.'

'But why choose Mr Bhatnagar's device?' asked Agatha.

'Honestly speaking, I didn't know anything about him at all,' said Miss Buchanan. 'Chemistry isn't my field. But out of the exhibits I could get information about, theirs seemed to be the biggest. I thought if they removed it or even just scaled it down, there would be more room for other people.'

'Yes, but Mr Bhatnagar and Mr

Mathur worked hard on their exhibit too,' said Christie. 'It's not fair to make them give up their space, either.'

'Well, it's just through that door over there,' said Miss Buchanan, pointing. 'I put it in the boxes I'd brought the snake tank in, but I did it very carefully. I don't think I damaged it at all. It should be fine to just switch them back again. I would appreciate some help with the glass case, though. It is awfully heavy.'

'Er, yes, of course,' said Mr Bhatnagar. 'And I *am* sorry that your applications keep being rejected like that. If there's something I can do to help ...'

'No, bless you, please don't worry about it. Thank you for being so kind after all the trouble I've caused for you.'

'Erm,' said a small voice.

They all looked at Agatha.

'Er, actually,' said Agatha, shyly, 'maybe there *is* something you could do. Something everyone could do. Um, Auguste, what do you think?'

She gestured to the row of tables and the exhibits displayed on them. The Belgian boy frowned, took a step back, then nodded his head. 'Yes,' he said, 'I think it can be done. There is enough space.'

'Enough space for what?' asked Miss Buchanan, mystified.

'Enough space for everyone's exhibits, if everyone shuffles their things up a bit,' said Agatha. 'I think, anyway.'

'I believe Aggie is right,' said Auguste. 'Not all of the exhibits take up a whole table and while some of them might need extra room for safety reasons, I think you could easily create more than enough space for your case of snakes.'

Miss Buchanan bit her lip. 'I'm not sure I deserve it! And would they all be willing to do that?'

'Nobody respects a scientist who is working purely for their own self-interest,' Mr Bhatnagar murmured to himself. Then, more loudly, he said, 'Don't worry, Miss Buchanan. *I* will persuade them.' He paused, smiling at the children. 'That is to say, my detectives and I will persuade them.'

The children beamed.

CHAPTER TWELVE

The children and Clara had a wonderful rest of the week in London. They visited museums, art galleries, the zoo, and even the Tower of London – as tourists, not prisoners, thankfully. Ada proved to be a great source of recommendations and even managed to get them all tickets to a Sherlock Holmes play.

The highlight of the week, however, was definitely taking their mother and Sir Conan Doyle to the Royal Society Summer Science Exhibition.

When they arrived, Mr Bhatnagar and his colleague Mr Mathur were chatting happily away with Miss Buchanan. The three scientists explained their exhibits to them and answered the visitors' questions enthusiastically.

'Oh, how interesting!' said Clara. 'So this is one of the most sensitive machines there is for measuring magnetic properties? It must be so useful for research and industry, too.

'And exposing snakes to ultraviolet light might have beneficial results? Goodness, me!'

'Thank you so much again for helping this all to take place,' Mr Bhatnagar said to the children. 'It certainly wouldn't have been possible without you.'

'And thank you for helping to get my exhibit included,' Miss Buchanan added. 'I really don't know how you persuaded them all! It's like a dream come true. Oh! Do you have your book for me to sign?'

Christie proudly offered it up.

'Here's a note I wrote for you, too,' said Miss Buchanan, as she gave the book back. 'Since you asked about swamp adders, I did a little research and wrote a list of real snakes that are potential candidates. Although, maybe I needn't have bothered, given you have the world expert on swamp adders with you.'

Sir Conan Doyle coughed and looked away.

All too soon, their week in London was over. Ada insisted on coming to the station to see them off. Poor Ada! It was sad to leave her behind. Agatha thought she would have followed them back to Devon if she could!

While they were waiting on the platform, Ada asked Christie, 'So what *did* Miss Buchanan write in your book?'

Christie held it out to her. Inside was written:

To Christie, my biggest fan.

Thank you again! I hope you continue your interest in snakes, while I will do my best to stay on the right side of the law!

Regards, Henrietta Buchanan.

'All's well that ends well,' said Ada. 'Congratulations, you two! Another successful case for the Parker twins. Everything is nicely wrapped up.'

Apart from losing my lovely new fountain pen, thought Agatha. But if Ada had forgotten and the others were blissfully unaware, she didn't want to bring it up.

'Yes,' said Agatha, forcing a smile. 'Thank you.'

At that moment, the train drew into the station. The children and Clara got ready to board.

'Goodbye for now,' said Christie.

She had a feeling they'd see Ada again, whether she liked it or not!

'We'll miss you,' said Agatha, giving Ada a shy hug.

'Me too!' said Ada. 'Oh! Almost forgot. This is for you.' She thrust a small package into Agatha's hands. 'Don't forget to write!' she said with a wink.

It wasn't until the train was steaming off to Devon that Agatha had a chance to open Ada's present. Christie, Auguste and Clara looked on curiously as she unwrapped it. When she unfolded the final crease, Agatha gasped aloud.

There in front of her was the wonderful fountain pen from Mr Einstein. Next to it was written, 'Luckily, Sir Bully has very loose pockets! Love, Ada.'

Agatha smiled. Perhaps things were nicely wrapped up after all.